A COMPLICATED WAY OF
BEING IGNORED

A COMPLICATED WAY OF BEING IGNORED

THE BEST NEW POETRY

2012

EDITED BY
MICHAEL STEWART

Grist Books 2012

Editor Michael Stewart

Cover Design Mark Savage

Inner Page Design Carnegie Publishing Ltd

A Complicated Way of Being Ignored is published by Grist Books.

Please note that all work published here is previously unpublished.

www.hud.ac.uk/grist

Grist Books is supported entirely by The University of
Huddersfield and would not exist without this support. We would
like to take the opportunity to express our gratitude for this
continuing support.

ISBN: 978-0-9563099-2-1

University of
HUDDERSFIELD
Inspiring tomorrow's professionals

CONTENTS

3 a.m. PHONE CALL

The call in the night and the frozen word
as you haul out of sleep on the splintered board,
punches your chest and worms into your brain:
you will never be anyone's daughter again.

YOU'VE SAT ON YOUR PHONE AGAIN

On the other end of the line
(you don't know I can hear)
bus times are being announced, loud and clear.

Your chair creaks; I know that'll be
you rocking back on its legs.
Your voice is a distant hum
as you make other women laugh.

You're drinking espresso with them,
as you did all last week in Brazil
while I waited at home for your call

sipping metallic wine
alone in this hollow house
watching branches rock in the breeze
on the other side of the pane.

SWEET NOTHING

Me: black woollen blazer, dandruff, Lennon specs,
briefcase with left-wing stickers, my initials.
I walk the playground's edge at Roundhay School:
off games, I'm on an errand for a beige-
shirted teacher who sometimes lends me books.

Them: the fighters have de-mobbed: the footie's over.
The truants, smokers, yobs have run for cover.
No lighted match is flicked; my hair's not pulled.
No amorous mad-girl tries to make me blush.
No stone is thrown from behind the laurel bush.

I am alone. Around me, nothing happens.

I try to take it in. I feel as if I'm stealing.
I do not know, when older, how beguiling
That static moment's memory will seem.

DEAR JARED

I feel as if I'm a failure as a step-parent
and I lament your having gone off Club Penguin
when you play Call of Duty (certificate 18) for hours
and then glibly describe how
you won the round by stabbing an enemy
in the head.

I felt as if I was a failure as a step-parent
when it was my turn to cook your tea
and I could not summon the resolve to persuade you
to have carrot and cucumber sticks
with your ketchup and salad-cream covered
chicken-burger.

I feel as if I lack the gravitas my father had
each time the pejorative terms I coin
about you fail to have any impact or,
what's worse, make bad behaviour take on a mystique.
Your consumption of coca-cola has not diminished
since I called it
the Devil's wee-wee.

And my parents would never have caved-in
as I did, when you complained you did not 'get'
your maths homework and eventually,
instead of trying to explain it another way,
I heaved an internal sigh and just told you
all the answers.

And I worry a great deal about your development
because you are worse at finding things than
anyone I have ever known, and your lies
about, for example, what happened to those *Breakaways*
always seem to involve ninjas or blue dragons and are
implausible.

But when I asked you if the underpants
you were wearing were the same as yesterday's,
without asking, you borrowed my pet phrase and said
'I won't say a word until I've seen my solicitor.'
When you spoke those words,
I stopped being your stepfather
and became your dad.

THROWING MOTHER
IN THE SKIP

Those seven colanders have had their day;
so has her dirty, old DAB radio.
The Dorothy L. Sayers books can stay.

Chuck the willow-pattern saucers, glass ash-tray,
but not this case of vintage red Bordeaux.
Those seven colanders have had their day.

These scratched-up vinyl albums just won't play.
The Oxfam shop can have these videos.
These fifteen Robert Heinlein books can stay.

I've found another case: just Vin du Pays.
This steamer and these pudding-bowls can go.
Those seven colanders have had their day.

Put her wedding-ring and trinkets on eBay,
but keep this case of Beaujolais Nouveau.
The Daphne du Maurier books can stay.

This tapestry is showing some decay.
I think this pulpy mass was "Cheerios".
Those seven colanders have had their day.
The Dorothy L. Sayers books can stay.

TRAMPS

First the one who hung around the gate,
his small, dark eyes like those of a vole,
tongue a pink sweet in his mouth.

Next the one with the Rasputin beard, black coat.
He peered through the kitchen window;
kicked at nothing in the air.

And then the one I found in the hall,
Christmas Eve. *Don't you remember me?*
This is my house, he said, and swayed a little.

PRESENCE

Birthdays and Christmases, you used to make
our presents. Late at night you'd be outside somewhere
sawing, planing, soldering – a doll's house for me,
shoe-box square and got in through the flat roof,
a grey Mobil garage for my brother.
A wooden sledge with runners which went rusty,
so heavy it just sank in the snow. A creaky swing.

We were unimpressed. They never matched the bought
things we'd had in mind. After bed I'd hear you talking
through design points with mum and sometimes,
on cold afternoons, I'd come into the shed
and peer deep into the paraffin heater,
loving its ring of flame and purple fumes.
Hoping for nothing, but that you would turn round.

POSSESSION

(on revisiting a second-hand copy of Adcock's *Twentieth Century
Women's Poetry* signed in green felt-tip *Elizabeth Scully or Scally,
Hebden Bridge*)

It falls open first at Plath then Adrienne Rich,
the sections between flapping back and forth at me
in virginal blocks. Spinster and Lady Lazarus
have been scribbled on or 'annotated' in the same
heavy hand, a pencil as thick as the pen.

Well it's mine now, Elizabeth Scally or Scully,
so I get a rubber, clamp the page under my left arm and rub
out *1962*, a line from Spinster to girl,
universal, cultural position of women,
a ring round Nazi lampshade, promise of *feminine
empowerment,*
AND THAT'S ALL SHE IS, make them pay, in control of the image
and some kind of plumbing diagram round O*ut of ash I rise.*

Now, Adrienne: *focus is now on the woman in the poems,* three
strange Masonic triangles, *waster,* and *cf Baudelaire or TWL.*

Next, break the spine at Mew, Bishop, Cope, Rukeyser,
Guest – Plath by now of course falling apart – and read
some. Let's hear it for them.
And Eiléan Ni Chuilleanáin,
whom no one round here talks about for fear
of mispronouncing.

There, all of you. A level playing field.

TRICK OR TREAT

Everyone knows it's true. Razor blades
slipped into apples, temazepam capsules
masquerading as jelly beans, used needles
introduced into liquorice pipes. Someone
who works in Environmental Health
told a friend of my cousin that people
hollow out Mars bars, stuff them with cyanide,
mix heroin in lemonade powder,
lace love-hearts with digoxin.

A professor of criminology investigates,
publishes his findings. Without a scrap of evidence
he concludes that nobody poisons children for fun,
nobody would take that much trouble
with nothing to gain. But the myth persists.
Everyone knows it's true. Police forces
issue warnings, hospitals X-ray sweets while
disgruntled kids wait, slavering for sherbet fountains,
avid for aniseed balls. Some parents keep
their darlings at home at Hallowe'en because,
whatever the experts say, everyone knows it's true.

Mrs Potts stirs potions in her kitchen. This
is the one night of the year when she can pay
them back: the apple-scrumpers and door-knockers,
the nasty child who tied a tin-can to her cat's tail,
the ones who trampled her dahlias, put dog-poo
through her letterbox. When they choke
on her arsenic fudge, they will have only themselves
to blame. Because everyone knows it's true.

TONSILLECTOMY

You'll be going to theatre presently, says the Virgin Mary.
It's Dick Whittington: there's a poster outside
Woolworths.
An ice-cream man presses a sieve over my nose,
and I can smell cherry Spangles. And then

I'm lying in a high white bed and they tell me
I've been to theatre, but I don't remember seeing Dick,
or his cat. No presents, either; just a bowl of ice-cream,
so at least the man didn't let me down

but I can't swallow it. My Mum isn't there; just angels
with squeaky shoes and swans on their heads.
Then Mum comes in for half an hour, says
it's all she's allowed; but she's brought me

a bag of liquorice toffees.
The navy-blue angel snatches them out of her hand.
These can go in the tin! Mother says
it isn't fair, she didn't mean for me to share them
with the ones who hadn't any

and I tell her about not seeing Dick and his cat,
after they promised, and she says she'll be taking it up
with the authorities, and they haven't
heard the end of this.

THE STUBBORN MAN'S FOOT
CARE ROUTINE

Hard to reach his toes these days;
has to sit on the bathroom stool,
grab one ankle, haul it across his knee.
The nails are cracked: a smoker's nails, he thinks.

The podiatrist embarrassed him
by lifting his feet on to the blue towel in her lap
as if they were precious, sweet-smelling baby feet;
not flaking tortoise-shell claws.

The ankle slides off his knee
before he has a chance to clip and file.
Soon his nails will hang over the ends of his toes,
click on the floor like an old dog's.

A PIECE OF TOASTED CHEESE

Much as I might want to take you
to Holy Island or to bed,
we'd only end up sore or sorry.

You are too smart to be that disingenuous;
I don't believe you, he said.
Self-serving narratives are rarely true.

Spare me the re-sprayed explanations.
Not since Jesus, Cicero or Rumi
has the human narrative changed.

Trivialities make the biggest difference –
bacteria in a petri dish, an icy runway,
a night to remember or the longest day.

THE SHELF LIFE OF
A CRISP

for Lesley

A crinkled membrane,
like a pharaoh's ear;
entombed in an air-tight bag:
its fate is usually cut and dried.
The shelf-life of an average crisp,
whether baked or fried,
is four months, five months,
no more than six.
Slightly longer than a foetus
in the land of potato-eaters.

Though we have but half
the time of an average crisp,
our fate is neither transparent nor opaque.
The shelf-life of our love,
fried or half-baked,
depends on us.

ONE MAN'S MEAT...

One man's gain
is another man's loss.
One man's fool
is another man's boss.
One man's raft
is another man's cross.
One man's gold
is another man's dross.

One man's sword
is another man's plough.
One man's 'can't'
is another man's 'how?'.
One man's beef
is another man's chow.
One's man's lie
is another man's vow.

One man's love
is another man's pain.
One man's drought
is another man's rain.
One man's bond
is another man's chain.
One man's blood
is another man's stain.

IMPORTED GOODS

When she moved onto the street
she brought a wilderness with her.
After van loads of sofas, fridges,
standard lamps and bed frames
came pots of oak, sycamore,
wild garlic and bluebells.
She brought a tea-chest full of rooks,
an Ali Baba basket full of rabbits,
a shoebox full of voles and dormice
and a little stream,
patterned with streaks of minnow fish,
that she rolled out on the pavement
like a Turkish rug.

After a month her terraced house
was thatched with a mesh
of honeysuckle and ivy,
birds were building nests
and laying eggs in her guttering,
emerald moss had cladded
her drainpipes
and a small woodland had grown
in her 6 foot yard.

Generally
the other residents of the street
were sweetened by the sight of butterflies
brightening the tired beige washing lines,

kingfishers flashing on the dustbins,
skulks of foxes glowing outside the corner shop
or Forget-me-nots growing through the concrete
but for some who were used to
nothing but the early morning roar
of traffic on the flyover,
the babble of the street
and the fat dawn chorus
were too much
and they complained about the noise
to the council.

CAMOMILE TEA

Your cottage always smelled
of wood smoke, turps
and old baked beans.
Washing up was a rare event
and the cabaret was mould.
Your good intentions
grew furzy blooms.
Things in pans developed skins.

You cooked but hardly ate,
lived on the wonky G note
you scratched and bowed
on your battered violin,
sucked fat from the colours
of the same raw-eyed siren
you painted every day.

Back then
I was doped up on camomile tea
and the idea of love,
unable to see the mess
behind your eyes.
thinking I'd saved a man
from drowning.

WINGS 'R' US

Yeah, like, Dad's always been, like, an airhead, right?
Drives Mum nuts. All his wacky get-bling-quick schemes.
Latest's gone pear-shaped – as per. So we gotta fly.
I mean, literal, man. He's been hoarding loo-roll tubes,
lengths of elastic, bits of candle for, like, weeks.
Oh, and taking this weird interest in, like, hens.

I mean, all he's gotta do is gimme the nod.
I txt some of the gang to, like, ramraid us outta here.
But Dad always has shedloads of, like, conspiracy theories.
Latest is this king fella we just done this
garden re-design for?
(Kindofa neat maze for some truly wild beastie of his.)
Anyhow, now Dad says that Mr-Crown-guy
wants to pop us.

So, like, we're gonna wing it. Sounds groovy.
Straight off this big fucker of a cliff.
Wish I could invite the guys, y'know,
have a few spliffs, a crate of Stella for the big off.
But Dad's reeeeal into his wacko groove:
strict Need To Know basis.
Mum's skyped to say "humour him".
But he's all yak-yak in my face!

Zeus! Less of the instructions already, eh Pops?
You'd think I was the airhead around here – duh!

GRAYSON PERRY

The dust-print
of spread-eagled sparrow
on the new double-glazing

The bee shaken in jamjar
by sweaty 8-year-old hands:
a dazing migraine of fear

The pentathlon's chest pushing
out into the universe that is beyond
the un-ribboned line

The potter click-clack-tottering
past the National Portrait Gallery,
rucksack pulling at his dahlia-print dress-strap

WE ARE SORRY FOR ANY INCONVENIENCE CAUSED

Were you man or woman;
drunk or ice-cold;
open-eyed and calm,
or screwed shut and shaking?
Were you swearing or praying;
facing direction of travel,
or driver?
Did you change your mind
but it was too late,
or scream the train on
because it was late?
Did you leave a quick note,
or throw all 32 attempts away?
Was it a loving gift to yourself,
or a punishment for Them?
Did you think there was no way out,
or decide not to take the ways?
Did you google to see
how effective a method it was?
Did it thrill you that many live?
How did you sleep last night?
Did you picture the people
who'd pick the pieces of you up?
Did you consider the driver?
Did you wonder if he'd
had a 'jumper' before?
Did you believe people who said
suicides are selfish?

Did you classify it into:
before / during / after?
Did you draw a graph of your pain?
Was it worth it:
For you
For the driver
For Them
For the people who picked up your bits
For those who were sorry for any inconvenience
For those who were inconvenienced
Was it a giggle a gamble a drunken stumble a revenge
attack a hate crime a sin a plea all of these?
You may have ticked more than one.

BEHIND HIS EYE

He keeps her in a bricked-up cupboard
behind his eye,
eclipsed by business meetings
and after work
squash tournaments.

She is Aphrodite's swan,
an ensnared deer,
the sirens' song.

She is an Arabic arabesque,
a Viking-plated she warrior,
Virginia Woolf.

She is home-baked bread,
figs savoured on satin sheets,
an unwashed teacup.

She is Lolita with one shoulder bared,
Rosa Parks,
Alice Herz, Jocelyn Bell.

A mermaid with a cunt
but no legs to run,
a martyr with chest agape.

He keeps her in a bricked-up cupboard
behind his eye.
But one day, between morning appointments,
she will claw her way out and soar
– a spiral of doves around the sun.

EVERY BONE

One day I come home to find
the sofa is no longer big enough.
When he was seven, we made buns together,
sprinkled silver strands on top
because hundreds and thousands were too babyish.
These days my hair's like that – flaked in silver.
My hairline recedes in an unwomanly fashion
like rolled-up turf at the end of the season:
his reveals a row of tiny pustules
and a frown that rarely breaks –
funny how, in Reception,
his self-portrait had the widest smile.
I see his father in him, the sulky part
when asked to wash up, or pass the mustard or,

well, anything. After days of not bathing,
I smell his father on him and try to remember that
all princes were monsters once.
I attempt to love every bone of the monster
but he bowls his Oedipal hatred at me
and I am afraid I will be petrified by it
or dissolve under its acidity. So I dodge it
and look the other way. He's taller than me now
and, whenever I turn around, he's there,
like a poltergeist trying to prove its existence.
I'm disappointed he hasn't yet learnt
that presence has sod-all to do with size.

He swaggers from reciting
one hundred and sixty eight digits of Pi
to weeping over a bee his friend stamped on.
I marvel at how both these things
make me feel closer to him and yet further away.
For the first time, I look – not into his eyes –
but at their surface. I see my flaws distorted there;
it is as though this is the first accurate mirror
I've come across
and I am older and uglier than I thought,
twisted up like plaited bread or a corroded school gate,
stretched to such an extent that I take up
almost the whole of his eyeball.
This morning I argued with him and he told me,
with the most gentle of gestures,
that I shouldn't have spoken to him like that.
He was right:

I have come home to find the sofa is no longer big enough.

IN PRAISE OF THE OFFICE CLEANER

Her gimlet eyes rake papers on desks and cabinets,
seek a way in.

Her bony hands have feathers, so that the merest touch
on bookcases and rows of Forms and Precedents
leaves them spruce.

Her bottom on the partners' chairs
fetches up a shine of walnut.

When she sneezes, she disinfects the telephones.

When she laughs, the skin of dust on monitors
splits its sides, falls away.

One brassy stare from her
and all the door knobs and name plates
come up gleaming.

When she speaks, her words rinse and bleach the air;
or, in more caustic mood, cut like oven-cleaner.

Her nose diagnoses problems in the fridge.

Her knees like loyal housemaids,
bend to serve the god of Hygiene.

Her breath leaves scent of parma violet
in all the rooms she passes through.

Her feet plant order on the doormats,
print a welcome in the lobby. Her hair

sweeps the floor.

WE MADE ANOTHER WORLD
IN YOUR KITCHEN

Tonight, I played that videotape
of us playing Astronauts. Costumed in clingfilm
and pipe-cleaner antennae,
with bedsheets and torchlight
we made another world in your kitchen.
Our spacecraft whirred like the microwave
as we rocketed past tin-foil satellites
orbiting dinner-plate planets.
We helmeted ourselves with colanders;
floated upside-down
in the concave of spoons. Removing
the moon from the fridge,
you threw a mozzarella ball at me: 'Contrary to
common belief, Buzz, the moon is made from buffalo milk.'
I threw kitchen-tissue asteroids
at your head. You turned to the lens
with waxing eyes,
and spoke your best robot voice
into a parmesan grater: 'Er,
Huston?
We have a problem.
We've run out of polyroll.'
I paused the tape there, just as you blinked
those coconut skin eyelids.
The screen started rolling
the way old tapes do. And
your body turned transparent.
You turned wraithlike.

A phantom spaceman. Perhaps,
by pretending to be in another world,
you became otherworldly.
I rewound the tape. Just
ten more minutes, I told myself.

LOVE IS NOT

an Apple MacBook – non-slip, sleek,
birthday gift-wrapped.

It's nothing in cellophane, nothing sporting
a designer label.

It is not intricate, can't be purchased
from a website touting All She Ever Wanted.

It neither tastes of chocolate nor smells of roses.
It cannot be daubed on the insides of wrists.

It is definitely not bosom-enhancing
and it isn't made of leather.

Love is not a lifestyle choice, nor a ticket
nor a dream of something not yet hatched.

No, love is that bottle of window cleaner,
acid-blue, half-empty, standing on the shelf,

that only now – rattling out a poem
on my clear, unfettered screen,

noticing the crisp, black type,
the total absence of fly-shit –

do I realise you used to clean my clunky laptop
I didn't even know was dirty.

FIRST LITTER

She birthed the first by a puddle
on the path, looked surprised

when I scooped it up, laid it gently
in the cushioned nest we had prepared.

The second, third and fourth appeared
without ado, moist as figs, lolling

in her thick brown fur, her tongue licking
their slick backs, sealed eyes,

tiny paws with claws like angel-hair,
the limp commas of their tails.

We watched her cup herself around them,
nudge them into life, her purr steady as milk,

pupils dilating as they squirmed,
latched on. Later she moved them

to a thread-worn blanket under our bed,
fetching them one by one across the warm pine floor.

I lie awake at night – your left arm slack
across my belly, mapping hollows,

your fingers draped against my hip
– and listen to them: the tiny mews, the break

and draw of suction, the hum of instinct
suckling in the dark.

DAY OF REST

She skates through the house
collecting saucers and spoons
like pebbles from a frozen lake.

From tables to mantels her fingers flutter
while we slouch over the Sundays.

Sometimes the hum of Ravel's Bolero
can be heard above the vacuum's drone
or the dishwasher's drum-roll

as blade marks carve through the carpets, past
snow-drift in forgotten corners –

and when we gather round the table,
her apron twirls as she turns
to serve our favourite roast

but no-one has the grace to raise
a perfect 6.

FROM UNBEAUTIFUL THINGS

Hugger-mugger with death, you cut out
like a Doodlebug descending in silence
through the luminous fug of air
to the debris already embedded in us.

The words at your last gasp were sounds that,
like all things great and misunderstood,
should never have to be heard for a first time –
how finely the lights get limed in the end.

We simple souls came to fill the temple
shedding tears in late November.
I saw anxiety as an unwreathed rose.
I saw the fingers of a new-born child
cradled in a mangled hand, and catch-lights
from the window quiver in a cynic's eye.

LEAVE OF ABSENCE

For the workaholic couple,
being off, sick, at the same time
is a togetherness of sorts,

although they'll quickly bore of each
other's worn and mithering care:
their under-the-weather chill-pills

can neither kill the need for a
materialistic fix, nor
fill their barren hope of a child.

Feathering an anvil.

And as they hammer vainly on,
they cannot live without themselves,
so riveted inside a world

that is too much with them, that is
at the same time held at bay, despite
the growing rust in every weld.

They claim iron constitutions
but the steel is in their gazes,
and the gazes at the abyss.

PARK VIEW

Dust of blizzard smothers the land
soon whiting-out meanderers

wind-whittled twists in snow-bestoled
arms: young bucks; sad philanderers;

heel-draggers; pandering mothers;
the wan face of an iron knight –

blessed alike for their investment,
weightless in the weight of pure white.

Taking flight for Dublin or Doone
and Western Lands, for the stalling

heartbeat and billowing soul, to
undertake a hermit's calling

and comprehend some new last end,
even in the faintest falling.

THE BOATS

Fishing fleet settles on shingle
Like old broody hens settling on sterile eggs of stone
Shedding feathers of paint, and memories.
They sigh with the wind, and a frayed rope beats a tattoo.
In the night they talk,
Recall the great days, of full holds and record catches;
Of early dawns, and storms ridden out
proudly against the odds.
Where are our skippers now? They mourn,
What did we do wrong?
And they sigh with the wind,
and a frayed rope picks out a lament.
Mine died, murmurs one.
His lady came, put her hand on my stem post
Cried and left forever.
Mine was lost at sea, mutters another
I turned back into the gale at the touch of the helm
They praised me for doing my best
It wasn't my fault.
And they sigh with the wind,
and a frayed rope taps out a dirge.
Mine still comes breathes another
The son of the son of the father.
He sits in the wheelhouse for a while
Then shakes his soft white fist at the sky
Curses a god called EU quotas
Curses a god called fuel prices
And sobs as he leaves.

None of it was our fault.
And they sigh with the wind
and a frayed rope sounds a drum roll.
A wave, more adventurous, lifts their sterns
Did you feel that? The sea, the sea!
And for a moment they move and live
But the tide lets them down
And they settle on shingle
Like old broody hens settling on sterile eggs of stone.
And they wail with the gale, and a frayed rope thrashes out
 a danse macabre
As the barometer drops to hell breaks loose
And the spring tides lick their lips.

ENCHANTMENT

They watch through the mesh
as my husband pumps me.
I stare back, dead as taxidermy and just as mean.
Our home is lined with words
on strips and ripped up pictures,
bleeding black tattoos when wet
with rain or my husband's urine.
Sometimes I chew on dangling strands
of piss- and rain-laden words
but my husband tends to forage
inside my mouth before I have a chance to swallow.
He's using his teeth as a vice to clamp me still
while he drills into me at high speed,
spitting up sawdust. *She's giving us the evils,*
they laugh out of their doughy faces, soft enough to slash.
Today, they've thrown roses, marigolds, dandelions and
sweet-smelling herbs over our shit.
Sprigs of basil float in our bowls.
He climbs on my head to pinion me with his claws.
He vibrates against my face.
After he's sprayed his scent in my fur,
he bows deeply beneath me,
expecting tenderness for hours.
I dream of gnawing through wire
and wood. I dream of biting the hand that grooms me.
As I bury my tongue
deep into his palpitating skin I dream of violence.

And what is she dreaming of,
the one who's exchanged her fur for my flesh?
What is she imagining
as she licks my stripy scarf and inhales the leaves
I left brewing in my pot?
What do my friends make of it,
now that the smallest of things give me pleasure:
my own set of keys, my waterproof coat, my pen
and most of all the sound of my voice,
which must have made her look like she'd been caught
in the headlights the first time she heard it and knew
it was hers, for speaking and singing and protesting?

HOW TO KEEP A
SKELETON KEY

Take nothing but one slice of bread
from the first house, spread it with butter
from the next, dress
in clothes stuffed in plastic bags
curled up by bins. Your new life begins.
Sleep in attics. Spy through cracks
in doors, scavenge down the backs of sofas,
when reading inscriptions don't snap the spines
of books. Look at wedding gifts stored in cupboards,
drink leftover wine. You'll see the tiny maps of gravy,
the dried-up wood lice where they keep
their sharpened knives. Slit no ladies' stomachs,
cut no throats, sell no babies
on the internet, feed pets. Restlessness
will take you to jewellery stores
and flower shops. On ocean liners,
in locked-up ballrooms, save yourself
the first waltz. Moonbathe along deserted decks.
On scorching days a butcher's meatsafe provides relief.
In bitter weather stroke discrete restaurant
cats. Find the names of unborn children
on the backs of lost receipts.

He might watch scraps of himself
glitter in the poem in his hands,
might understand why his past
plays out in films and books,
might need to look behind curtains

before he goes to sleep,
might remember it's been years
since he piled up your possessions,
they keep the landing grim,
crammed under the pull-down ladders;
he only meant them there a day or so
while he rearranged his life.
He won't do anything about the stink.
He'll just get used to it.

THE MOMENT

On the Penistone train derailment, February 1916.

When I look up at the seamed sky,
the black teeth of girders, the cracks of fresh air,
I think this is not an accident, but a moment
of refusal, a point I can look on and describe
in bricks of words, then knock down again
before it becomes too fixed,

      not an accident
but a pause, a determined holding of breath,
a gap into which all thoughts pour,
about how the world crumbles, how men
stand aside, watch as it all slides
easy as coal slack, the cold hearts

      of their pocket watches
ticking against their ribs, as things sink
under their own weight, how broken things lie
on their sides for as long as it takes
for someone to call for help, blow a whistle,
wave a red flag,

      how this moment is the result
of one small fissure where rainwater crept
into stone and, in freezing, filled its own lungs
and pushed permanence aside.

WHAT I KNOW

That the roots of lycopsid trees have the span
of a giant squid, that their bark is patterned
like the skin of a pineapple or a globe artichoke,
that ex-mining towns rest on their fossilized remains,

that beneath the tangled gardens of West Street,
with stained mattresses slumped against privet,
heaped remains of old bathrooms, carcases
of kitchens, beneath mossed patches that might be lawns,

deep down in the seams of the earth, the wings
of the first dragonflies, the flattened shells of crabs,
lie imprinted in coal, along with the thigh bones
of tyrannosaurus rex, which hold evidence

of air sacks, the pneumatisation that enables
birds to fly, and here in these towns where everyone
is someone's cousin twice removed,
we are all breathing through our bones.

SHIRLEY, IT WAS YOU

Your black hair curled at the fringe,
your painted nails, the second-hand Astrakhan
that swung from your shoulders.
You were walking down Kilburn High Road
towards the market where you used to work.
Your shoes were too high, like they always were.
The money belt full of change weighed at your hips,
made you sway like a belly dancer.

In the distance, I could see your husband,
the man you married after divorcing the first.
He looked exhausted, but you hadn't changed
at all. Perhaps it was the sun, rising
between buildings, lighting the slice
of pavement you were walking on.

CENTURION

I checked the nails, three straight, one spare.
The hammer. The helmet. The spear.
Eased the hasp to allow jab and stab.
Stiffened like steel in the early morning starch.
Baulked at the still wet caulking.
Listened for the dead man labouring
under the weight of the last piece
of his life's puzzle.

Such an arrival!
The noisy tide spilling up the sweet hillside
rolling its tortured cargo up and up
to my very feet.
And then the task.
Mounting the wretched carcass on its canvas.
Silence but for the hammer strokes
and the faint cry of the breeze,
a sudden weeping sky
and a guilty twist of trees.

The hours dragged.
Only the clatter of dice relieved the monotony.

Strange at the end.
He seemed to have fused with the wood.
All a homogenous red.
As if we had created something.

SENSIBLE SHOES

Being descended from a long line of clickers and cloggers
It was in my genes always to wear a sensible shoe.
Sandals to Sunday school,
Fur-lined boots in winter,
Buffed black leather for Market Street or funerals.
(All measured by Clark's special contraption).

But by the time I reached the removes
My feet had aspirations.
Why should they be Jennings
While the rest of me was Jagger?

I bought winklepickers,
So streamlined, so tight,
I walked out of the shop like a geisha.
To show off, I wore them to school.
They got wet and curled into medieval toe-ends.
I watched them unfurl through double maths.

Corns grew on the inside of my toes.
Is fifteen too young for bunions?

There was only one advantage.
On the break-time kick-about,
I could hook the ball into the bike-shed goals
From the craziest of angles.
I had prehensile feet,
And for the first time ever,
I could dribble better than Bucko.

A HERMIT WITH A
PARKING PERMIT

Below the cones of orange street-light,
in drizzle beside damp tarmac
a man without a face, hood-up.

A parking permit around his neck,
unshaven, his shaky hands
come out of his pockets
and his fingers dance slowly with the rain.

A man who had forgotten his name,
remembered where he parked his car,
an old rust-bucket down the road,
that clanged when driven
was clamped when not hidden,
and a steering wheel wet with spittle.

This was his home,
and on it he'd cook eggs,
on a hot day,
using the bonnet.

When he drove, he would go anywhere
and he didn't care much for traffic lights,
until the time he sped through amber
and side-swiped a lorry loaded with timber.

HOW AN OLD MAN LEAVES
HIS LIFE-LONG WIFE

Earlier that day,
they sat on each end of the bench
by the beach, eating in silence yet again,
her pickled doorstep sandwiches.

As the tide retreated and the clouds emptied,
the mist closed in;
the remnants of their marriage
which, like the rain that day,
had been falling for years.

Each drop pattered and danced
upon the planks of the pier,
like they used to do here.

She was the first to sigh
when they got up to leave for home,
as he ignored behind
using the umbrella as a leg.

That night – before the day he left –
she remembers finding him
downstairs on the couch
laughing into his glass of red,
in between his nicotine lips.

She saw him caress the neck
and sigh
before each pour
from the bottle's intoxicating grip.

She hugged her gown around her
and went back up to bed.

The morning after when he awoke,
he pulled his trench-coat over his vest
and brushed her on the cheek and said:

"I'll be in my tool shed,
spraying pesticides onto my cigarettes."

THE MUSK OF THE
FULL MOON

She's waxed to the sheet in the flush of a burning moon.
Juggernauts shudder a flimsy bedroom blind
and zeros flickering on a fierce clock-radio dial
seem jeering. She kicks off the quilt. Toys strewn
across the floor commemorate a child
recently perished in a pool of lonely
midnight sweats, a girl whose lost balloons
are prowling the sky, reverted to the wild,
streaming the ribbons that slithered out of her grip:
cherry bubbles wrinkling down to prunes.
The lunar month is peaking as she gropes
naked for a coat to cover herself.

Truck drivers' horns are trumpeting wolfish tunes
as she flutters across their path, a flighty sylph,
the hint of a wisp absorbed by dark woods.
Oaks enclose her. Shaggy ink-caps push
their fists through leaf mould. Maidenhair ferns enmesh
her hips. Branches poke and snatch at her hood.
As a little girl she loved the trees
but now at night she squirms, ill at ease,
sensing the needling stares that converge on her country
raincoat probe her soul. She feels awkward.

He sniffs the breeze and draws towards her scent.
A relic of an older world, not ghost,
not myth, just flesh and blood misunderstood.
Her mum and dad, she knows, would be aghast
but the moon is a gland, stinking out the sky,
streaking leaf and bark with daubs of shine.
The watcher grunts to make his presence known.
She stiffens, swallowing a reflex cry,
eyeing his bulk, the bestial, muscular person
emerging from the murk between the trees,
the restless hoofs, the tiny ammonite eyes,
the rapier prong on his snout erect and fearsome.
But he trots through the glade with a faltering lope,
halting submissively at her feet, shyly
laying his leathery muzzle in her lap.

The night is subdued
    while the musk of the full moon lingers
and the creature sleeps, cheek nuzzling her thigh,
mollified, tusk enfolded in her fingers.

PERHAPS PRAYING

At this moment the knives of rain
spark from her nose and cut into the screen.
Her arms are spread, her mouth a dark wound,
her fingers knotted, knuckled into fists
tight against the grey.

I want to reach through to her armouring rags,
all bark and rust, to hold not fix those ruined hands
and promise the rain will stop one day, it must.
Such arrogance, perhaps she has prayed
for this for an age.

A ZOO IN TUNISIA

A lioness was goaded from her cage.
A line was scratched, and there she flopped
like a sack of wrapped tools.

We were asked, "qui voudrait le caresser?"
My hand seemed to raise itself.
I stepped, crouched, brushed
her doormat-flank,

and felt the salt heat of breath,
as dark eggs of eyes turned to me
with the reluctance of a fallen woman.

VAN GOGH'S OTHER MISTRESS

When she smells their daughter's fresh citrus scent,
oranges fill her mouth and throat,
sweet from Arles.

When their son's hair strokes her cheek,
she savours ice-cream melting, vanilla
sunflowers on her tongue.

When his whisper brushes old promises,
she hears his ear unspiral, her teeth crunch on bone.
She tastes nothing but paint.

WHERE?

The proper place for a secret is not the dust
under your valanced bed or the back of a wardrobe,
even if locked. The family closet is not discreet.

You may try wrapping it in layers of tissue
placed in a small bag, sewing this into your heart,
smooth and seamless, before stitching closed
your mouth.

You might fold up its flesh inside a steel box,
then bury this at night: some soil-smothered grave
at the bottom of a garden overgrown with weeds.

But those bones will give it away, even as it rests
stiller than earth in the hollow of your skull
beneath this wasteland with its bramble chains.

Some dog, some badger will smell it and dig it up.
This is fact. See how your speech, your eyes,
your twitching hands already reveal it.

IN THE WAITING ROOM

a man with a loose filling
is waking from a dream

it is a dream of a man drilling
through the roof of his mouth

it is really a man drilling
through the wall

you would think a dentist
would have the plumber in

out of opening hours

THE SMOKER'S TABLE

The table surface is a universe of
coffee halos that spirograph the cheap mahogany,
a collage of orbits
linked and bound ringlet chains.
The mapping of a conversation and a brew.

The ashtray mounds a field of stumped corpses,
charred remains of a smoke
buried in a grave of ash.
A litter so vast you could almost smell the coughs
and apologies
that hung over the flicker of a match.

SCANNING

You were going to scan a document, you said,
rising from bed in the dark.
While the light scanned
your lips sought the punctuation marks of my body,
the frost-hard nipples, the scar of my belly,
the soft, downwards point,
moving backwards and forwards.
I don't know how the scanner sees,
or what sixth sense you use
to find geography in the dark.
Is that you or the machine humming?

SHEDDING

First I lost my umbrella.
It was bright green, foldaway,
with a wonky spoke.
Left behind in the toilets,
on a shelf above the basins,
but I didn't go back.

My single leather glove
was a full stop on marble.
I kept on walking.
My red coat was shelved
in the overhead locker
as I sprinted from the plane.

My bag was different; stolen
by a man with a moustache.
I panicked then; no money,
no cards and no identity.
But I had air in my lungs,
and sun on my back.

I lost my taste for egg and chips,
callied with paella
but my tongue sought out
plainer fare; the grittiness of sand
and the tang of sea salt,
which was heady when inhaled.
I lost my lowered eyelids,
could look waiters in the eye.

My body lost its straightness,
it curved onto beach loungers.
My legs were languid, my
fingers rippled the turquoise sea.

I lost the first layer of
skin in the swimming pool,
came up clean as shining bones.

Crossing the tarmac to the plane,
I was the one with no shadow.
I sat in my seat, then
vanished down the crack of it.

LEO

She follows the dog's gaze
to the top of the spiral stair
where he used to appear, upside down,
fair hair brushing the step
each morning.

She wanders the house.
No cushions piled on the floor for trampolining
or for dens from which to view The Lion King.
In the kitchen, she makes boring grown-up food,
no doors bang. No through draughts.
The garden is empty.
No one swings from the lowest branch
of the apple tree.

The scars on the grass from sliding tackles
are starting to heal.
Only a few caveman drawings
of motor bikes and aeroplanes
decorate the mantelpiece
and a fat yellow ball perches
high in the apple tree
like fruit.
Like the sun.

THE ÉCLAIR

I sat. Oldish, greyish, dull. He leaned into the space
opposite, unloading from his tray a cup and saucer
of orange tea and a plate with a bulging-luscious-chocolate-
glistening crisp-pastry-crackling-white-cream-oozing éclair.

He sat fatly, picked up the éclair and lifted it to his wet lips.
I saw the wide dark pink inside of his mouth stretch as he
bit, chocolate sticking to yellow teeth, eyes squeezed shut to
focus the ecstasy.

I shut my eyes too and pictured the young hunk sitting
opposite me, dark, wiry hair, intense blue eyes watching
me as he lifted, licked, tasted, then blew the last puff of
cream to me – like a kiss.

VISITING THE PARENTS

Here is the heavy weather.
There will be highs and lows throughout the day,
But the threat of disapproval will remain constant.
Veiled comments will be frequent,
And taking the moral high ground common.

Coasters will be widespread,
And surface covering continuous.
Wind will be gale force at times,
But hilarity zero.

The son will set off at 6.30pm,
Followed by clear skies
And calm seas.

ARNOLD JACOBS' FLAWLESSNESS

'Arnold Jacobs was the Paganini of the tuba'

Paragons of the tuba would discuss
the legend of Arnold Jacobs' flawlessness.

I listened as the silver band rehearsed
in the Temperance Hall. It waltzed

and spun. It sobbed
and moaned. It swabbed

the historical air with bleats.
I noticed this

though I was young
and careless: that it sung.

Since then, of course, we all have
faltered. Love,

for instance. Literature.
The less than seemly embouchure

attempted in the service
of ecstasy and grace.

The seasons cycle on. They solemnize
and sing the days and Arnold Jacobs is

eternal and precise,
still garlanded in praise

among the sheds of heaven
where the past is lain

to rest in fields of stars, his song
the antiphon of antiphons.

GLASS BOTTOM BOAT

Neither sea-sickness nor curfew swayed me
worming through the rectangled crowd;
their faces scaly and Bridlington blue.
Rogue elbows and wrecking ball breasts
knocked any question out of me reaching the front
where I swear I saw a mermaid nursing her
lover's skeleton still wearing flippers,
goggles and snorkel.
No one noticed me vaulting the barrier
but when I started stamping on the glass platform
adult hands hooked my oxters
reeling me in kicking and flailing
before I broke through.
Afterwards, curled up in a pile of coats,
my mother peeled back my ears to reveal
the gills I had drawn with her eye-liner
pencil.

THE PASSENGER

Pigeons:
stretched out on the sky between towers
like dice spots.
I try to keep that Kodak moment
before they're behind the buildings,
on an arc to intercept
the poorer end of town. Somewhere
around the great glass bulwarks
of the city they have a home, are homing
on the need of that same, safe world,
insistent under the odd sky that smells wrong
the way salmon smell the sea and find
it's suddenly foreign.

I try to count them in my memory
and wonder if they understand the numbers,
if they might decide to go astray,
fly up from the baskets until out of sight –
and then cut west, to hide out in the fug
of some small bar, hunched
over the old corny, samey
must of home.

The plane is down and makes an arc
in the pavane around the runways.
Formalities: immigration, customs,
taxi out into the spaghetti of the map,
and I'm picking at the knot that says

its just the same, the same again,
drizzle and the brick-kiln smell
and the random spots of rain
on the ravelled suburban river
that I haven't stepped in once.

THE HORSES IN
THE DARK

We do not see them whole. Stair-rods
of rain have welded them onto the banks
in the dark. The horses are all gods,
black sparks and zigzag rivers on their flanks,

the rain welding them into the banks
of the carriageway. They stand along the route,
black sparks and zigzag rivers from their flanks
the only light beyond the absolute

of the carriageway. They stand along our route
oblivious to the rain and the car,
the only life beyond the absolute
pouring tunnel of headlights and tar.

As if they didn't see the rain or the car
the horses have gone deep into their weight,
the pouring tunnels of headlights and tar
mean as little as the bridle or the gate.

The horses have gone deep into their weight.
They make no sound. Our beams of vision
mean as little as the bridle, the five-bar gate
is a joke, a thought in the wrong dimension.

The horses make no sound. The swerve of vision
less than a raindrop in the world they bear.
It's a joke, a thought in the wrong dimension
to call them ours to own or ride. They stare

at less than a raindrop in the world they bear
against the spheres of darkness. Beyond a name
to call them ours to own or ride, they stare
through rain so hard the gutters cannot drain.

Through rain so hard the gutters will not drain
we cannot see them whole. Stair-rods
pummel against a darkness beyond name.
In the dark the horses are all gods.

FULL TIME

Each Wednesday night we'd meet for five-a-side.
We won 2-0 the week his mother died.
I guess we find our peace in different ways.
There were no prayers or tears,
but he cleared a couple of chances
off the line.

Then, at full time,
we didn't talk it over.
Just an awkward 'sorry'
with a firm hand on the shoulder.
And for his second pint
I paid the two pounds, twenty pence.
We won 2-0.
He played, as ever, in defence.

BIRD

On the landing I stood watching the bird,
its small chest moving only slightly now.
Taken from the mouth of the family cat
it lay, feathers ruffled, wings akimbo.
Then my mother sighed and tried to explain
what the stillness meant, what death meant in words.
"But why?" was the only question I had.
I thought of the mohair coats that she wore,
one turquoise, another red like plumage.
And with my ear pressed to her chest she asked,
"Are you afraid that will happen to me?"
From then on I would walk to her wardrobe
just to pull down those coats from their hangers
and sit. Wearing one, smelling the other.

MUSHROOMS AND
OTHER FUNGI

Every evening at the top of his house,
he places No Entry on the door,
takes up his horn-handled knife,
slices deftly into cap and stalk.

Sulphur Tuft. Dryad's Saddle.
Scarlet Elf Cap.

Prompt at seven he eats
his supper alone in the damp dining-room,
plans his notes,
chewing slowly.

Beefsteak. Oyster. Poison Pie.
Jelly Babies.

Fifteen thousand already
catalogued in his neat banker's
hand, under their discrete headings.

Edible. Not Edible. Hallucinogenic.
Deadly Poisonous.

September, the driest in twelve years.
His investments are sound, but not
a good year for the Edibles.

Chanterelle. Fairy Ring Champignons,
Parasol. Deceiver.

Alone at the kitchen table his wife
planning a clean break
checks her list.

Keys, passport, money,
tickets, suitcase, letter.

Unnoticed
their children,
growing in the dark.

TUMBLER

"I've had a fall," she says, and I find I'm shocked more
by her turn of phrase than the accident itself.
My first thought is to question why
she has not more simply said, "I fell."

It's 'old lady' talk to turn it around this way:
she did not fall, it seems a fall was 'bestowed'
upon her as she tried to cross the road.
The loss of agency makes her sound frail.

But there's pride in her voice: that people came
to help her in the street. She's thrilled and wears
calamity like a badge. I'd swear she's glad
it happened: it proves that someone cares

and comforts her, while her Son only picks her up
on each new loss of footing in her speech.

A KIND OF BLUE

Art wears a pork pie hat,
a scrap of goaty beard,
is learning the scat,
and the names of the modes.
He even knows the notes
in one or two of them.

Art is currently practising
smoking grass without coughing,
drinking gin without gipping
and the baritone sax slouch.

He has the blood of a dancer in his heart
but not in his legs,
the soul of a poet in his head
and the voice of a singer
who sleeps noon-till-noon

He's in with the in-crowd
in his own room.

TRANSPARENCY

Water, someone said,
has a glint of the supernatural.

The glittering dots which fleck out
every pint of it

catch the sun
like spores of Heaven,

reflect on
the insides of themselves,

and light always seems to gather
on one part of it:

a finger,
pointing to a river –

THE SKY LANTERN

It is an empty apparition but it glows –
slowly sinks so as to be recognised –
a white balloon, the spirit
flying up inside.

Crumpled ghost, it passes here tonight,
falls to where the world can see –
watches and waits and drops
whilst burning

out cold in a messy sheet, or tipped into
a fire-ball – setting ablaze a year of corn
somewhere so far from here
they kneel to the sun.

THE DAY YOU LEFT

The day you left
plates dashed themselves
from the cliff of the dresser.
The cupboard door
left ajar, and like a child
I cannot resist a peek inside.
But no shiny parcels live
amongst the shattered china.
I keep the cupboard locked
but not bolted.
On certain days I sneak
the key and peer inside.
It's been too long now:
one thousand, three hundred
and forty two days.
Yet still, each souvenir is kept
intact, in pristine condition.
Memory encapsulated
in amber like prehistoric DNA,
a kiss blown and caught
palm against cheek,
I pin it out with all the care
of an amateur lepidopterist.

FIVE BLACK CROWS

She took a voodoo doll
a squashy foam filled thing
a novelty shop find,
it looked nothing like him.
On hands and knees, prostrate, praying,
muttering oaths like a latter day saint,
she combed the spare room carpet
for his crepitant toe nails
She shook scurf from soiled sheets,
collected relics of their disunion.
She raided his clippers for decaying
bristles, dust to dust, ashes to ashes,
enrobing the doll with a litany
of misdemeanours.
By the light of the moon
she sang her missa solemnis.
Sharp pins through the eyes, the groin,
his chief members of sin and greed.
But for the heart – ah, for the heart –
she selected a skewer,
a six inch steel stiletto,
one he'd used to barbecue kebabs,
whilst sending messages
to his latest object of desire.
She heated it in flames
in sight of the goddess.
When it glowed
hot enough to melt human flesh

she pierced his heart.
It yielded easily,
singeing cloth and foam
with an acrid burning.
She buried him beneath the elder,
the long spike protruding
from pitch black soil,
marking the place of burial
like an ancient cross on a barren moor.
In the morning she saw snowdrops
pushing through the loam
and five black crows
dancing on his grave.

ABOUT THE AUTHORS

Jacky Tarleton

Jacky lives in Devon and is studying for a PhD at Exeter University, exploring Louis MacNeice's poetry through the lens of Gaston Bachelard. '3 a.m. Phone Call' won the Huddersfield Festival Poetry Competition in 2010 and 'On Saturdays Father Wrote Sermons' was recently runner-up in the Poetry Society's Stanza Competition.

William Thirsk-Gaskill

William Thirsk-Gaskill is the lost love child of Ted Hughes and Alan Bennett. He writes verse to experience a sense of achievement. He loves distasteful details over palatable abstractions. He lives in an unfinished house with two related faces of the letter J. His blog can be ignored at: http://iamhyperlexic.wordpress.com

Rosie Blagg

Rosie Blagg was born in the West Country in 1983 and has lived in Leeds for the last nine years. She is studying for a Psychology MSc and volunteers at Leeds Survivor Led Crisis Service. Her poems have been published in magazines including The North and The Interpreter's House.

Julia Deakin

Julia Deakin was born in Nuneaton and teaches at the University of Bradford. The Half-Mile-High Club was a Poetry Business Competition winner and her first collection, Without a Dog, appeared in 2008. Widely published and broadcast, she has read on 'Poetry Please' and won four first prizes in 2011.

Nina Boyd

Nina Boyd lives in Huddersfield, where she writes poems about mad women and sad children, and dabbles in fiction. She was the overall winner of the 2009 Poetry Business Book and Pamphlet Competition. Her first collection, Dear Mr Asquith, was published by Smith/Doorstop Books in 2010.

Jim Greenhalf

Jim Greenhalf's remaining days on earth – 4,000 to 8,000 at a guess – will be spent, hopefully, making the best of the legacy of the previous 23,000, mindful of the Law of Un-foreseen Consequences and the part played by sanctimony and hubris in the daily struggle to acquire grace under pressure.

Gaia Holmes

Gaia Holmes lives in Halifax. She is a free lance writer who works throughout the West Yorkshire region. Gaia's first poetry collection, Dr James Graham's Celestial bed, was published in 2006. Her second poetry collection will be published by 'Comma Press' in Spring 2012. In her spare time Gaia is a DJ for Phoenix FM, Calderdale's community radio station, and also bangs big drums at gigs and rehearsals with Sambalifax.

Char March

Char March is a multi-award-winning poet, playwright and fiction writer. Her credits include: five poetry collections, six BBC Radio 4 plays, seven stage plays and numerous short stories. 'Wings 'R' Us' is from her latest collection: 'The Thousand Natural Shocks' (pub. Indigo Dreams). www. charmarch.co.uk

Becky Cherriman

Becky is a commissioned writer, creative writing facilitator, and prize-winning performer based in Leeds. She works regularly for the Workers Educational Association, The West Yorkshire Playhouse, Artlink West Yorkshire and Ilkley Literature Festival, develops writing-related resources for The Hepworth Wakefield and is currently penning a magical realist novel.

Geraldine Clarkson

Geraldine Clarkson started writing poetry four years ago. She was awarded an Arvon/Jerwood mentorship with Jo Shapcott and chosen for Writers' Centre Norwich Escalator development scheme. Her poems appear in Smiths Knoll, Envoi, and This Line Is Not For Turning: An Anthology of Contemporary British Prose Poetry (Cinnamon Press, 2011).

Charlotte Walker

Charlotte Walker is a Poetry MA student studying with Carol Ann Duffy and Michael Symmons Roberts at Manchester Metropolitan University. Charlotte has also run literary events for the Albert Poets in Huddersfield, given poetry workshops and readings at the Elmet Trust, and taught screen-writing at Manchester College.

Sharon Black

Sharon Black is originally from Glasgow but now lives in the Cévennes mountains of southern France. She has been published widely and has won several poetry awards including The Frogmore Poetry Prize 2011. Her first poetry collection *To Know Bedrock* is published by Pindrop Press. www.sharonblack.co.uk

Tim O'Leary

Tim O'Leary is a photographer, former archaeologist, and recent recruit to poetry. Apart from Grist, in the last year he has been commended/shortlisted in Ireland at Strokestown and the Munster Literary Festival, and in Italy at Poetry on the Lake. His work has appeared in Word Gumbo and Poetry Salzburg Review.

Nicky Summerson

Nicky was born in 1949 in Kent. After school she studied and worked in horticulture. She moved to Devon with her husband in 1993 and began writing short stories for fun. She has been writing poetry for 3 years. The Boats is her first poetry competition entry.

Josephine Corcoran

Josephine Corcoran writes poems, plays and short fiction. Some of her work has been broadcast on BBC Radio 4 and performed at The Chelsea Centre Theatre, London, and is published in various places, most recently in the Bridport Prize Anthology, 2010, and on the webzine, Ink, Sweat & Tears.

Julie Mellor

Julie Mellor graduated from the University of Huddersfield in 1996. She went on to Sheffield Hallam where she gained a PhD in 2003. Her work has appeared in London Magazine, Mslexia and The Rialto and her poem, 'What I Know', was voted best Yorkshire entry in the Elmet Open Poetry competition, 2011.

Pete Ardern

Pete Ardern was born in South Cheshire in 1952. He spent his early years drifting from job to job – farmworker, platelayer, gardener before training to be an FE lecturer. He currently teaches refugees on a resettlement project in Hull, Yorkshire and is writing fiction for teenagers (the Bily Ingham series).

David J. Costello

David J. Costello lives in Wallasey, Merseyside, and is co-organiser of local poetry venues "Bards of New Brighton" and "Liver Bards" (the latter in Liverpool). His work has been published in several anthologies and poetry journals including *Quantum Leap*, *Reach Poetry*, and *Envoi*. He has been shortlisted and placed in various competitions, most recently winning the 2011 Welsh Poetry Competition.

Matt O'Brien

After I graduate from Huddersfield University with a degree in English Language and Creative Writing, I plan on winning the lottery, moving out of England before it becomes like 'V for Vendetta' and making sure that I never see a syntax tree again for as long as I live.

Tim Ellis

Tim Ellis is a gardener in Harrogate. Well known on the Yorkshire performance poetry circuit, in the same week as winning Grist he became York Poetry Slam Champion 2011. His two books are: Birds of the World in Colour (Flarestack) and Gringo on the Chickenbus (Stairwell) See his website: www.birdbard.co.uk

Steve Nash

Steve Nash is based in York, where he fills his hours as a visiting lecturer and PhD student at the University of York St John. His poetry has been published internationally and he serves as the current poetry editor of both Open Wide Magazine and Indigo Rising UK.

Graham Burchell

Graham Burchell was born in Canterbury and now lives in Devon. He has an M.A. in Creative Writing from Bath Spa University. His first collection 'Vermeer's Corner' was published by Foothills Publishing in 2008. His latest collection, 'The Chongololo Club', will be published by Pindrop Press in July 2012. www.gburchell.com.

Sarah James

Sarah James has won or been shortlisted in various poetry contests and published in Rialto, Magma, Poetry Nottingham, Orbis, Poetry News and 2012's Lung Jazz: Young British Poets for Oxfam (ed Todd Swift). Her collection Into the Yell (Circaidy Gregory Press 2010) won third prize in the International Rubery Book Awards 2011. Her website is at www.sarah-james.co.uk.

John Bosley

John Bosley was born 1937 in Stevenage and has lived in Huddersfield for about 25 years. He is an ex-teacher, ex-drugs worker, ex-ceremonies officiant for the British Humanist Association and, for now, an ex-poet – as he is giving short prose a go.

Suzanne McArdle

Suzanne McArdle was born in a British Forces hospital in Berlin and enjoyed a successful career in management before training as a life coach. Her poems and stories have appeared in national magazines and pamphlets. She wrote her first book aged nine and is currently working on her second novel.

Janet Wadsworth

An ex-boat-builder (narrow boats) I write. I've had thirty or so stories published, usually in small canal-based magazines, and one or two poems. I've self published a novel about brass bands, and sold the thousand copies which I had printed. And written two canal thrillers (not yet published).

Liz Holt

Liz Holt is a lecturer in English at Huddersfield University. Most of her publications are non-fictional: She is currently writing a book on the use of laughter in interaction. But she also enjoys writing stories and poems. She has previously published poems for children.

C J Allen

C J Allen's poetry has appeared in magazines & anthologies in the UK, USA & Ireland (& occasionally on bits of sculpture in the Peak District) & has been broadcast on BBC Radios 3 & 4. His most recent collections are: A Strange Arrangement: New & Collected Poems (Leaf Press) & Violets (Templar Press).

Matthew Stoppard

Matthew Hedley Stoppard was born and brought up in Derbyshire, but now lives in Leeds, regularly appearing on the Yorkshire performance circuit. He is a competition winner and features in Popshot, The Cadaverine, Dead Ink and Eunoia Review and forthcoming editions of Iota, Cake Magazine, and Message In A Bottle.

Ian McEwen

Ian McEwen is a charity trustee and online philosophy tutor. Many magazines have published his poems, including Smiths Knoll, Poetry Wales and Poetry Review. He is on the board of Magma. His pamphlet The Stammering Man was a winner in the Templar competition 2010. Ian lives in Bedford.

John Newsham

John Newsham was born in Bradford in 1989. In 2011 he graduated from Lancaster University with a BA Hons. degree in English Literature and Creative Writing. In addition to his passion for writing, John is also a keen musician and amateur rugby league player. He currently lives in West Yorkshire.

Matthew Newby

Matthew Newby is a twenty-two year old poet and saxophonist from Leeds. He is a graduate of the University of Hull, where he studied English and American Literature. He was awarded the 2011 LIPPfest Leeds Prize for this poem and is currently putting together his first collection.

Chris Raetschus

Chris Raetschus from South Wales, worked for the Foreign Service in Teheran, lived in Nigeria and Germany, was a College Lecturer in Northampton before settling in Northumberland where she was a Registrar of Births, Marriages and Deaths. She won the local Ottaker Prize, was published in Orbis, plus highly commended and runner up in various competitions.

Greg White

Greg White is a graduate of the University of Leeds. He is currently working on a collection of poems on the subject of his late Mother's dementia, of which 'Tumbler' is the first to be anthologised.

David Gill

David Gill is author of The Amateur Yorksherman, a bestseller for the legendary Redbeck Press. His songs have been recorded and performed worldwide by top jazz artists including Liane Carroll, Sophie Bancroft and Deborah J. Carter. He currently writes for the cult blues-rock jazzer Chaz T.

Charlotte Walker

Charlotte Walker is a Poetry MA student studying with Carol Ann Duffy and Michael Symmons Roberts at Manchester Metropolitan University. Charlotte has also run literary events for the Albert Poets in Huddersfield, given poetry workshops and readings at the Elmet Trust, and taught screen-writing at Manchester College.

Angela Varley

When Angela's not working in a library, she escapes to meander through woods, dawdle along beaches and lie in grass watching clouds. She is inspired to write by reading, having time to contemplate, being close to trees and water, making things with clay and papier-maché and engaging with visual art.